This is a
very special gift

_____

for

_____

from

_____

date

# Emily
## the Chickadee

# Emily's New Home

A True Story
by Carol Zelaya

illustrated by Kristin Metcalf

Emily's New Home
Copyright © 2008

Published by:
Richlee Publishing
17791 S. Nicks Place
Oregon City, Oregon 97045
Author: Carol Zelaya

Cover art and interior art: Kristin Metcalf

ISBN-10 0-9796265-2-8
ISBN-13 978-0-9796265-2-4

Printed in Singapore

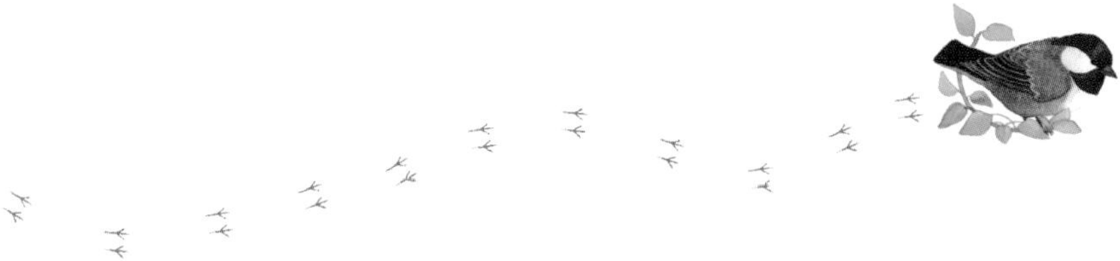

On a chilly Autumn day,

I had to move so far away

To the country, more room to play,

Near cows and horses

And barns with hay.

So why do I wish I could stay?

It's scary moving far away!

I miss my house and yard and tree.

I miss my birdie family.

How will they find me?

How will they know?

Especially in the winter snow?

Where do birds fly when it's cold?

Do they know our house was sold?

I miss my little Emily

And wish real hard for her to be

Outside my window, next to me.

There she would chirp so happily.

I'd watch her eat and drink and play.

Winter, please just go away!

Then one sunny springtime day

At my new house far away,

On the front porch I can see

Some twigs and straw in front of me.

They're in a pile upon the floor,

And sticking out of my front door!

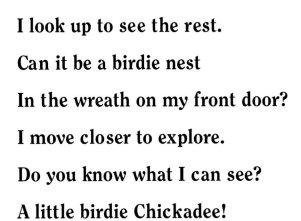

I look up to see the rest.

Can it be a birdie nest

In the wreath on my front door?

I move closer to explore.

Do you know what I can see?

A little birdie Chickadee!

Can this be my Emily,

My mommy birdie Chickadee?

She's found a dry and quiet place

In a cozy, comfy little space.

Safe and warm, up off the floor,

She flies from the nest

On my front door.

I'm as happy as can be.

It seems that she has followed me

To my new home far away.

I know she will only stay

To raise her birdie family

From birdie eggs…

All one, two, three!

She'll keep them warm,

Feed them every day,

Until they grow and fly away

From their nest on my front door.

Then she'll come back, just like before,

To make a home again near me.

My little Emily, Chickadee!

If you look closely you can see

Another birdie family

Will make a home right next to you,

And this is all you need to do:

Give them water and seed each day,

With lots of love, and they will stay!

The End

## About the Illustrator

Kristin Metcalf is an artist and avid gardener. She enjoys living in the Pacific Northwest where the region's natural beauty is a constant inspiration. Her studio is surrounded by many of the flowers found in these stories of Emily and the air is filled with bird song and squirrel chatter. To see more of Kristin's art visit www. metcalfstudios.com.

# About the Author

Emily's story is a true story. This tiny bird came to visit Carol Zelaya at her Oregon home and ended up staying for years . . . even following her when she moved.

Carol Zelaya was born and raised in Chicago , Illinois. However, it wasn't until moving to Oregon that she discovered her true love for nature.

Deer and birds were daily visitors, but it was one special little chickadee that inspired her to write. She named the bird Emily.

Carol has written Emily's story in hope of educating children about nature's precious gifts that are all around us when we take the time to notice.

Carol still lives in Oregon with her husband and dogs, surrounded by trees, birds and other wildlife. She loves to travel and write poetry, but it is nature and all animals that she is most passionate about.

There are two more books in the EMILY THE CHICKADEE series!

Look for:
CARING FOR EMILY'S FAMILY
EMILY WAITS FOR HER FAMILY

Please visit her at: www.emilythechickadee.com

# My Chickadee Log

## I saw a Chickadee!

Where was the Chickadee?_____

Did you see a Chickadee hop?_____

Did you hear a Chickadee's call?_____

Did you see a Chickadee eat?_____

Did you see a Chickadee fly?_____

Did you see more than one?_____

What time of year did you see the Chickadee?

Summer? ❏

Winter? ❏

Spring? ❏

Fall? ❏